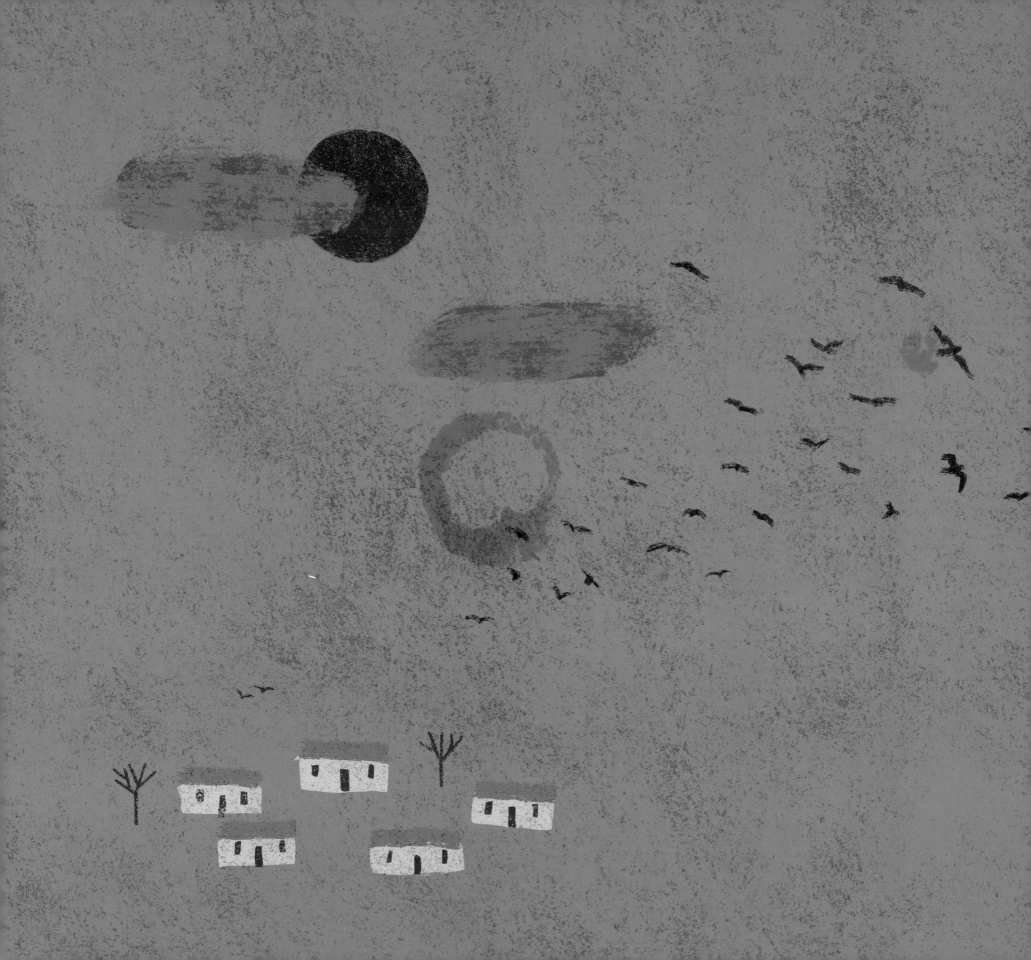

# Fly

BRITTANY J. THURMAN

illustrated by ANNA CUNHA

A CAITLYN DLOUHY BOOK

ATHENEUM BOOKS FOR YOUNG READERS | New York London Toronto Sydney New Delhi

Africa has a birthmark in the shape of her name.

In the classroom, down the hall, out the front door— her birthmark leads the way.

After school on Monday, she sees a poster that says:

Double Dutch Competition
This Sunday at Noon!
Meet Outside the Library

"What's a competition?" Africa asks her brother.

"It's when you show the world what you're made of," he answers.

That evening Africa declares to her family, "I'm going to show the world what I'm made of."

"Say what?" asks her mother.

"Come again?" says her father.

"Huh?" asks her brother.

"On Sunday I'm going to jump, fly, double Dutch to the sky."

Africa feels certain she can double Dutch until her shoes are in fast-forward, until her feet forget the ground, until she flies like the birds in the sky. She feels certain she can double Dutch like her grandma used to. Momma's told her that back in the day, not a soul could beat Nana's fast-moving feet.

"But, Africa," says her brother, "you've never double Dutched before. You can't do something you've never done."

Her brother has a point. Africa has never double Dutched.

That night, she tries to learn, all on her own.
"Move your feet."

"Focus. Focus. Focus."

"Step to the rhythm."

No matter how much she tries to learn all on her own,
Africa thinks there must be a better way.

As they get off the bus on Tuesday,
Africa whispers to her bestie best, Bianca,
"Bianca, teach me how to double Dutch."

"Never could." Bianca laughs.
"But I can show you how to dance."
Bianca jitters, jives, bounces to the side.
It's no double Dutch, but Africa joins her.

In art on Wednesday, Africa says to Omar, "Omar, how do you double Dutch?"

"Who wants to double Dutch when you can step?"
Omar says. Omar steps, one foot,
then the next. One hand, then the other.
It's no double Dutch, but Africa joins him.

At lunch on Thursday, Africa sees Kay and Laura.
"Hey, how do y'all double Dutch?"

"Can't do that, but we can do 'Miss Mary Mack,
Mack, Mack, all dressed in black, black, black.'
Want to join us?" Kay and Laura clap and sing.
It's no double Dutch, but Africa joins them.

At recess on Friday, Africa yells to Whitney, "Whitney, show me how to double Dutch!"

"Double what?" Whitney says. "Never learned. But I can double-cartwheel, double-backflip, double-somersault. Wanna see?" Whitney cartwheels, backflips, and somersaults.

It's no double Dutch, but Africa tries her best to join her.

During piano lesson on Saturday, Africa can't help but look out the window.

"Tomorrow, I'm going to jump, fly, double Dutch to the sky."

The next day Africa walks up to the poster that says
*Double Dutch Competition Today at Noon!*

"Africa," her brother reminds her, "you can't do
something you've never done before."
True. Africa has never double Dutched.
But now Africa knows how to dance, how to step,
how to cartwheel, how to sing, how to move her hands this way
and that—everything you need to know to double Dutch.

"Today, I'm going to jump, fly, double Dutch to the sky."

The jump ropes twirl as if
the two are becoming one.

Africa counts, "One, two, three."
Africa sways. "One, two, three."

Africa jumps—"one, two, three"—into the ropes,
moving her shoes in fast-forward, letting her feet
forget the ground, flying like the birds in the sky.
Africa double Dutches like her friends taught her,
better than her nana used to,
beating those fast-moving feet.

Africa has a birthmark in the shape of her name
that's always shown her what she's made of.

For Calise, Lizelle, Zamira. Soar!
—B. T.

To Carolina
—A. C.

ATHENEUM BOOKS FOR YOUNG READERS · An imprint of Simon & Schuster Children's Publishing Division · 1230 Avenue of the Americas, New York, New York 10020 · Text © 2022 by Brittany J. Thurman · Illustration © 2022 by Anna Cunha · Book design by Karyn Lee © 2022 by Simon & Schuster, Inc. · All rights reserved, including the right of reproduction in whole or in part in any form. · ATHENEUM BOOKS FOR YOUNG READERS is a registered trademark of Simon & Schuster, Inc. Atheneum logo is a trademark of Simon & Schuster, Inc. · For information about special discounts for bulk purchases, please contact Simon & Schuster Special Sales at 1-866-506-1949 or business@simonandschuster.com. · The Simon & Schuster Speakers Bureau can bring authors to your live event. For more information or to book an event, contact the Simon & Schuster Speakers Bureau at 1-866-248-3049 or visit our website at www.simonspeakers.com. · The text for this book was set in SimpleLife. · The illustrations for this book were rendered digitally. · Manufactured in China 1021 SCP · First Edition 2 4 6 8 10 9 7 5 3 1 · Library of Congress Cataloging-in-Publication Data · Names: Thurman, Brittany, author. | Cunha, Anna, 1985- illustrator. · Title: Fly / Brittany Thurman ; illustrated by Anna Cunha. · Description: First edition. | New York : Atheneum Books for Young Readers, 2022. | "A Caitlyn Dlouhy Book." | Audience: Ages 4–8. | Summary: Africa enters a double Dutch contest without knowing how to double Dutch, and on her journey to learn her friends show her how to jive, step, clap Miss Mary Mack, and do cartwheels. · Identifiers: LCCN 2020023148 | ISBN 9781534454873 (hardcover) | ISBN 9781534454880 (ebook) · Subjects: CYAC: Double dutch (Rope skipping)—Fiction. | Rope skipping—Fiction. | African Americans—Fiction. · Classification: LCC PZ7.1.T5455 Fl 2022 | DDC [E]—dc23 · LC record available at https://lccn.loc.gov/2020023148

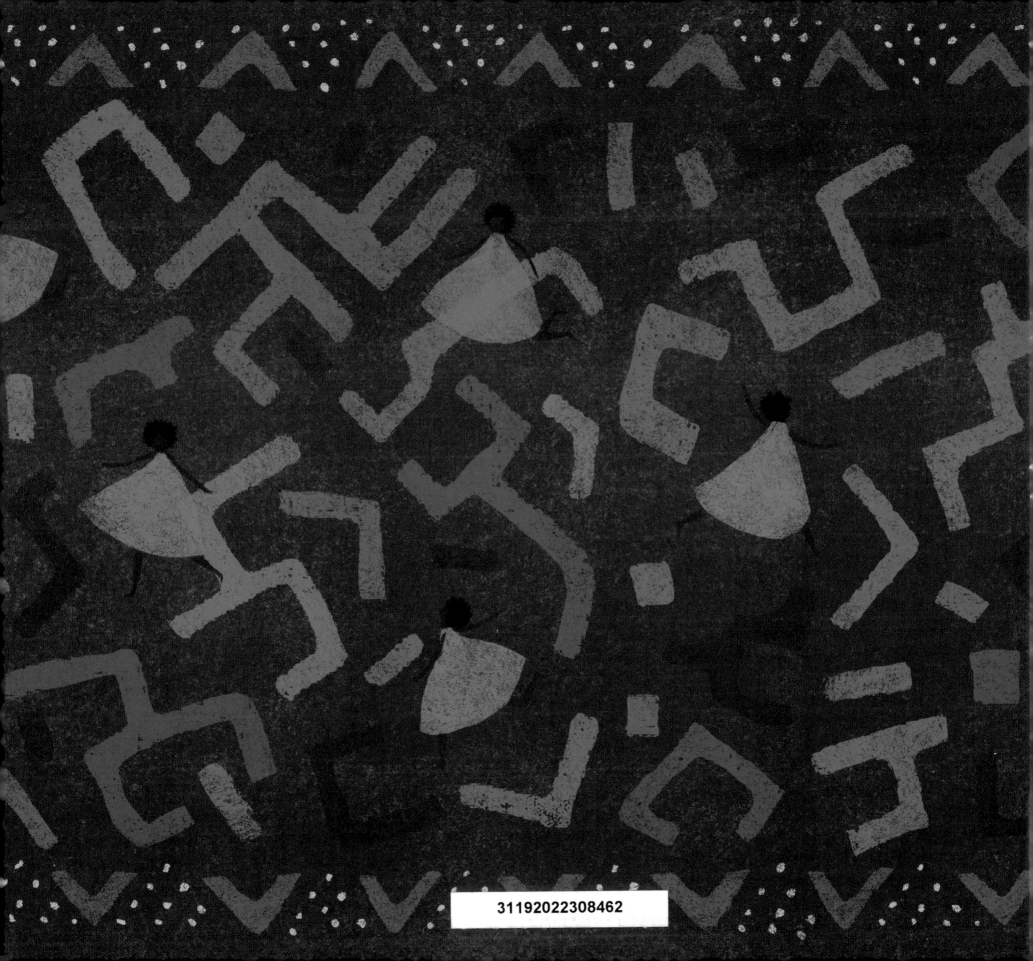